Cyril and Pat

Emily Gravett

Simon & Schuster Books for Young Readers

New York   London   Toronto   Sydney   New Delhi

Lake Park only had one squirrel,
all alone and sad (poor Cyril).

Until the morning he met Pat,

his new best friend, a big gray . . .

Pat and Cyril spent each day
thinking up good games to play.

They liked to put on puppet shows,
and test how fast a skateboard goes.

Their *favorite* games were hide-and-seek,

and one that they called Pigeon Sneak.

Shhh

Oh, Cyril, can't you see that your friend Pat
is not like you. Your friend's a . . .

Real joker!

At lunchtime, when the ducks were fed,
Pat jumped in and took some bread.

Oh, Cyril, can't you see that your friend Pat
is not like you. Your friend's a . . .

Brilliant sharer!

And when they both got chased by Slim,
together they outwitted him.

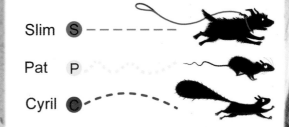

Slim S – – – –

Pat P · · · · ·

Cyril C – – – –

Oh, Cyril,
    can't you see that your friend Pat
is not like you. Your friend's a . . .

CLEVER SQUIRREL,
And you can't catch us!

shouted Cyril.

Pat tried to learn to earn a treat
like Cyril could, by looking sweet.

But no one threw a treat for Pat.

Urgh! Mom,
I saw a great big . . .

Oh, Cyril, can't you see that your friend Pat
is nothing but a dirty rat?

Oh, Cyril, can't you see that your friend Pat
is nothing but a *thieving* rat?

Oh, Cyril, can't you see it? Facts are facts.
SQUIRRELS CAN'T BE FRIENDS WITH RATS!

Cyril, now back on his own,
tried to play their games alone.

But when he tried to outrun Slim,
things didn't go so well for him.

Past the pond, and down the slide . . .
no time for him to try to hide.

Cyril RAN.
Out of the park,

into the city . . .

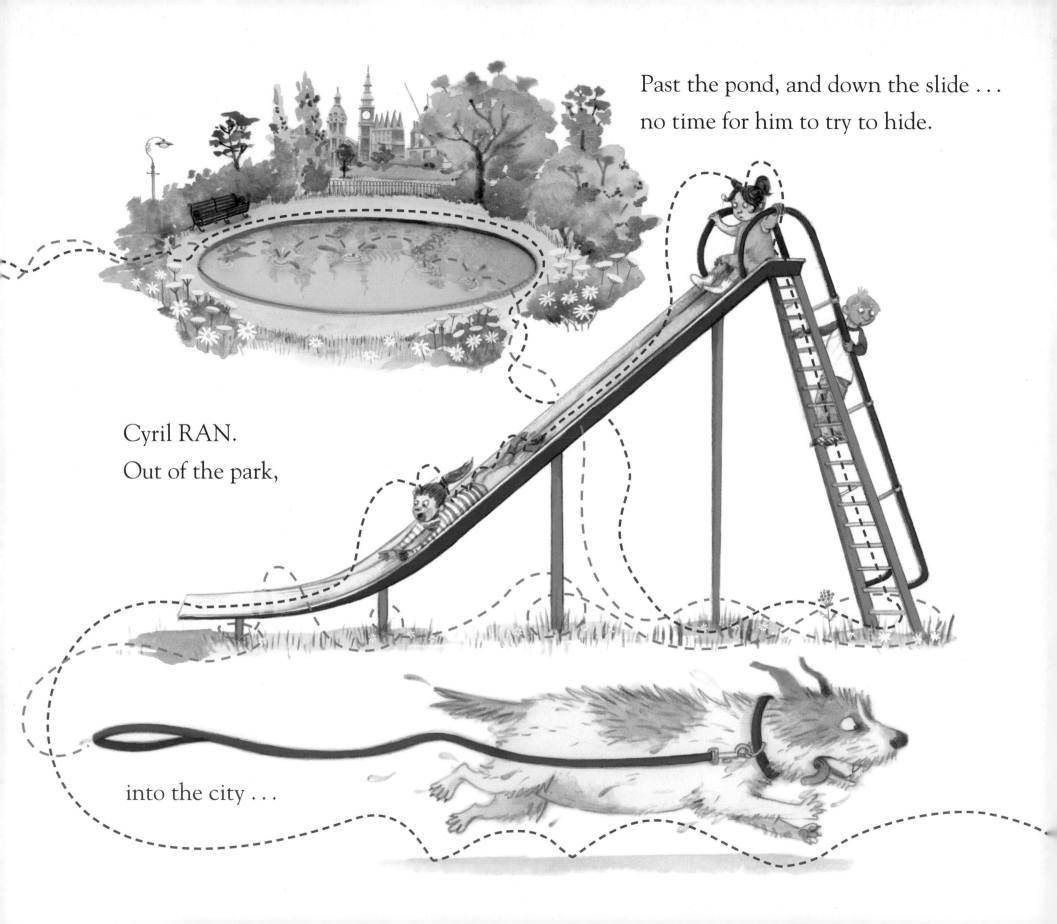

into the dark.

All alone and scared.

(Poor Cyril.)

Not *quite* alone, you stupid squirrel.
And *not so brave* without that rat.

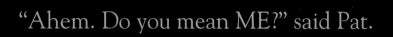
"Ahem. Do you mean ME?" said Pat.

Lake Park still only has one squirrel —
but he is not alone. Now Cyril
lives there with a large gray rat,
his brave and clever best friend, Pat.

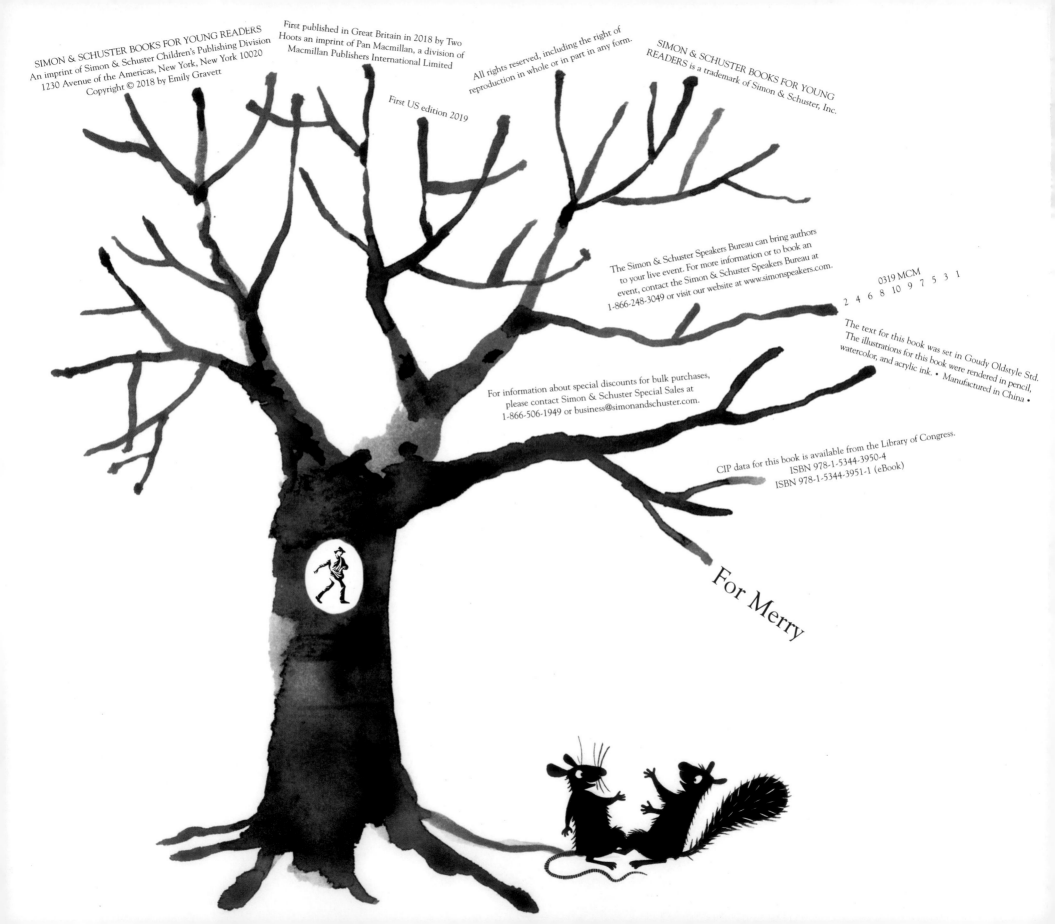

SIMON & SCHUSTER BOOKS FOR YOUNG READERS
An imprint of Simon & Schuster Children's Publishing Division
1230 Avenue of the Americas, New York, New York 10020
Copyright © 2018 by Emily Gravett

First published in Great Britain in 2018 by Two
Hoots an imprint of Pan Macmillan, a division of
Macmillan Publishers International Limited

First US edition 2019

SIMON & SCHUSTER BOOKS FOR YOUNG
READERS is a trademark of Simon & Schuster, Inc.

The Simon & Schuster Speakers Bureau can bring authors
to your live event. For more information or to book an
event, contact the Simon & Schuster Speakers Bureau at
1-866-248-3049 or visit our website at www.simonspeakers.com.

0319 MCM
2 4 6 8 10 9 7 5 3 1

The text for this book was set in Goudy Oldstyle Std.
The illustrations for this book were rendered in pencil,
watercolor, and acrylic ink. • Manufactured in China •

For information about special discounts for bulk purchases,
please contact Simon & Schuster Special Sales at
1-866-506-1949 or business@simonandschuster.com.

CIP data for this book is available from the Library of Congress.
ISBN 978-1-5344-3950-4
ISBN 978-1-5344-3951-1 (eBook)

For Merry